SPOOK SCHOOL

Curse of the Rat-beast

PETE
JOHNSON

Illustrated by
Tom Percival

I Turn into a Bat

It was a horrible slimy slug.

I concentrated hard and said, "Now, slimy slug, fly on to Lewis's nose."

The rest of the class watched the slug soar over to Lewis, who was so busy doing his homework he didn't notice it circling round him. It was only when the slug settled on his nose that Lewis suddenly shot up into the air.

"What's that?" he shrieked.

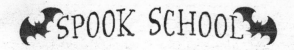

The whole class fell about laughing.
"You did this, Charlie," cried Lewis.
"Of course I did," I said.

I can make slugs appear out of
nowhere. And scary spiders. And
anything else, because I'm a ghost. So
is everyone else at this school. Only
we'd much rather you called us spooks.

I've only been at Spook School for a
few weeks, and to begin with it was all
pretty scary. All of us spooks hang out
in this huge, grey building surrounded
by fog. There are long, dark corridors
too, with thick cobwebs everywhere.
It's a bit like wandering into a horror
film, when actually, you're at school.

I wasn't too chuffed about having
lessons again, but here we learn

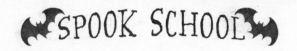

awesome stuff like how to fly and walk through doors and, of course, how to make things appear out of thin air. And tonight we were going to find out how to shape-change. I couldn't wait.

Our teacher, who's called Top Ghoul, began the lesson by saying, "You're each going to change into a small, brown bat. I want you to imagine you're looking at that bat now. Try to see it as clearly as possible in your head, then shout, 'Shape-change'."

We all focused on the bat, yelled, "Shape-change", and waited. Nothing happened.

"Concentrate harder," she said.

Now the room was so quiet you could have heard a cobweb fall.

"Shape-change!"
I bellowed, trying
really hard. And
suddenly, I'd done it.
I'd turned into a
bat. The first one
in my class.
The next spook to
turn into a bat was Lewis.
I was pleased about that, as
he's the first spook I met here,
and he's also my best friend.

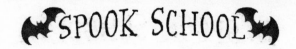

"How cool is this?" cried Lewis, swooping about.

"It's amazing," I replied.

Very soon the room was teeming with bats fluttering and diving about. "This is a top lesson, Top Ghoul," I said, looping the loop.

"Good," she said. "But that's long enough for your first attempt. It's time to get back to normal. Now all concentrate hard and say, 'Shape-change back'." She waited while we all changed back, before adding, "And I don't want any of you practising shape-changing out of my lessons. Is that clear? It could be dangerous on your own."

Dangerous! What did she mean by that?

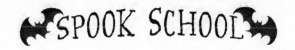

After lessons finished we all floated back to the dormitory, talking excitedly about the shape-changing. It was getting light and we should have been getting ready to go to sleep (yes, all spooks sleep in the daytime), when Paul, one of the other spooks, dared me to turn into a bat again. Soon everyone was daring me – except for Lewis.

"I just don't think you should," he said anxiously.

"But why not?"

"Because Top Ghoul said it could be dangerous."

I laughed loudly. "I'm sure she was just saying that to scare us," I said.

"No, honestly, I've got a bad feeling about this," said Lewis. "And you really

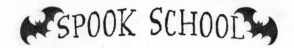

don't want to get into any trouble …
not when we might get a new mission."

A few spooks are sent to Earth to
investigate mysteries and strange
ghostly happenings. They are called the
Spook Squad. And Lewis and I are
members. Recently we had been sent on
our first mission – to find out about the
terrifying Mothman. No other spook
could solve the case, but Lewis and I
did. It had been pretty scary, but now
we were bursting for another mission.

I hesitated for a moment.

But then I said, "Look, Lewis, I'm
only going to shape-change into a bat
for thirty seconds. Nothing can go
wrong in such a short time, can it? Now
everyone be quiet while I concentrate."

"Actually, you're the one doing all the talking," said Paul.

"So I am." I grinned.

I decided this time I'd be a huge bat with a massive tail. I closed my eyes, pictured the creature really clearly and yelled, "Shape-change."

The next moment I was flying around the dorm. Everyone let out a massive cheer.

"I bet I'm a dead cool bat, aren't I?" I said, as I flapped and swirled at an incredible speed.

☾SPOOK SCHOOL☽

After I'd whizzed around the room about six times Lewis said, "Charlie, your time's up."

I'd been flying so fast I felt a bit dizzy so I was ready to stop. I cried, "Shape-change back." Only I didn't change. And instead, something terrible happened.

I kept on flying.

Chapter Two
The Dare That Went Wrong

Thirty seconds later I was still flapping
around the dormitory. Everyone
thought I was just showing off.

"Charlie, come down," cried Lewis.

"Shape-change back," I shouted
again at the top of my voice. But
nothing happened. I just went on going
round and round. It was like being on a
never-ending fairground ride. Everyone
was yelling stuff at me, too.

"Stop shouting," I gasped. "I can't stop and I'm feeling all dizzy." And then I did something really embarrassing.

I fired out of my bottom what looked like a furry little pellet. Only it was actually a bat's doo-doo. Everyone yelled and ducked as more bat's droppings shot out of me.

One even landed on Paul's head. "Urgh! Gross!" he cried, trying to pull it out of his hair; only he couldn't. "It's stuck on to me as well."

"It suits you!" I laughed.

"You did that deliberately," he yelled.

"Honestly, I didn't," I said, as I whirled round the dorm for the ninety-fifth time.

"I'm going to tell Top Ghoul what you've done," wailed Paul.

"You can't," said Lewis quickly. "We all dared Charlie to be a bat. We're all to blame for this."

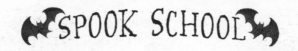
"Excuse me," I cried. "I'd really like to get down from here. Has anyone got any suggestions?"

"No," said Paul with a gloating smile.

"So we'll have to get Top Ghoul, won't we?" added Ray.

I was feeling so ill that I didn't argue.

"I'll go and get her," said Lewis.

"Well, hurry up before he fires any more bat's doo-doo at us," said Paul.

Lewis flew over to the door – but then stopped.

"What's the matter?" I asked.

He didn't answer. But the whole room had turned completely still. Someone was swirling into our dorm.

Only it wasn't Top Ghoul.

It was Spookmaster.

Chapter Three

In Big Trouble

There are scary teachers.

And very scary teachers.

And then there's Spookmaster: the head of Spook School. He looks like a very fierce lion … and that's just his normal face. But when he's angry an icy mist surrounds him. And right now, it was rising up around his feet.

Spookmaster glowered at me. "What is going on here?" he demanded.

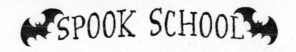

"Well, the thing is," I explained, "I was just going to be a bat for thirty seconds – but things went a bit wrong, as you can see." I gave a nervous laugh as I zoomed right past his nose. "And now I can't stop flying about."

Then, to my total horror, I let off another bat dropping. It landed right on Spookmaster's black cloak, with a loud splat.

No one dared laugh, although I knew they were dying to.

"Stop now!" he thundered.

"That's the problem," said Lewis. "He can't."

"Yes he can," said Spookmaster. "Charlie, look at me."

I turned to look at him, while still

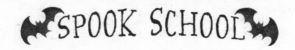

whirling frantically round the room.

"Now, believe in your power and say, 'I can stop now'," he instructed.

Still gaping at Spookmaster's stern, withered face, I said, "I believe in my power and I can stop now."

Well, I didn't stop but I definitely slowed down a little.

"Keep trying, Charlie," he ordered.

I tried again and again, and each time I slowed a little more. I felt like a clockwork toy whose batteries were running down. I became slower and slower until, all at once, I stopped moving altogether and hurtled down on to the floor. "That's a relief," I said.

Spookmaster glared at me. "Shape-change back at once," he boomed.

That part was easy compared to the flying part. A few seconds later I was my normal self again. I grinned at him. "Hey, that's better. Thanks a zillion, Spookmaster, I thought I was going to be bat-boy for ever."

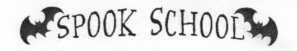

But he didn't smile back. And the icy mist around him looked even thicker. Then I noticed all my bat's droppings had gone too.

"Thanks for clearing up all my mess."

"You only made a mess because you got frightened," said Spookmaster. "And as soon as you got scared all your powers melted away."

"Oh well, no harm done," I said hopefully.

But Spookmaster replied in his fiercest voice, "You and Lewis to my room now."

"Not Lewis," I said, hastily, "he had nothing to do with it, honestly."

"Both of you to my room now," said Spookmaster.

With that he was gone. And Lewis and I had no choice but to fly after him.

We sped down the corridors. Although it was daylight outside, everywhere was as dim as a cave. "I'm so sorry..." I began.

"It'll be all right," whispered Lewis.

"No talking, Lewis," snapped Spookmaster.

When we reached Spookmaster's room, the corridor grew even darker. There was just one tiny candle flickering way up in the ceiling. Grey fog poured through a window too; it was so thick that the door seemed to appear out of nowhere.

Spookmaster floated through it and ordered us to follow.

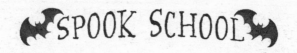

His room was like a typical head teacher's study, with a large desk and a comfortable chair for him and a very uncomfortable chair for any pupils unfortunate enough to be sent there. But today he didn't perch on his chair. He flew right up to the ceiling. So did the icy mist which now surrounded him like a low wall. "Top Ghoul told you not to practise shape-changing on your own, didn't she?"

"Yes," Lewis and I chorused.

"So, Charlie, why did you disobey her instructions?"

"It was a dare," I said quickly.

Spookmaster frowned. "Lewis, why didn't you stop Charlie?"

"He did try to…" I began.

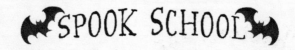

Spookmaster flitted angrily above our heads like a giant wasp. "I'm talking to Lewis," he said. "You're Charlie's friend, Lewis, and you've been here longer. You should know better. You should have stopped Charlie misbehaving and wasting his powers."

Spookmaster went on. "Do you know why I was floating past your dorm?"

"You heard us making a noise?" I suggested.

"No," said Spookmaster. "I was looking for you both."

Lewis and I stared at him.

"You weren't coming to tell us about a new mission, were you?" cried Lewis.

"Yes I was. But after today's misbehaviour, I've changed my mind."

Chapter Four
The Rat-beast

"But you can't do that," I cried. "You've got to let Lewis go. This had nothing to do with him."

"Oh no," said Lewis. "I'm not going without you."

"Stop this babble at once," roared Spookmaster, in such a loud voice all the cobwebs in the room shook.

"Sorry," I said, "but we're desperate to go on another mission."

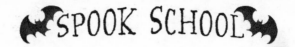

"I know that," said Spookmaster, "and I was very impressed with the way you solved the mystery of Mothman. But how can I trust you, Charlie? How do I know you won't start acting like a three-year-old and disobey instructions again?"

"Because I'm the new, improved Charlie, and I'll never, ever mess about again," I cried. And right then I really meant it.

"You'll never, ever mess about again," Spookmaster repeated after me, but I'm sure I saw a flicker of a smile cross his face. And the icy wall around him suddenly vanished. It was just a tiny, little cloud now. And then that floated up into the air and disappeared too.

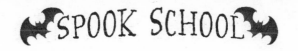

"You remind me of someone," said Spookmaster. "Of me, when I was your age." Another tiny smile crossed his face.

"I can't imagine you being like me – or me being like you," I cried, getting a bit muddled.

Then Spookmaster said something very exciting indeed. "Fly up a bit nearer," he said, "while I tell you about the case."

We didn't need telling twice.

"I want to tell you about a ten-year-old boy on Earth called Tim Webb. He is being haunted by a most terrifying ghost. One night he was in his room when he heard a strange chattering noise. At first he couldn't see anything,

31

but then he spotted the tiniest rat he'd ever seen scurrying across his bedroom floor. It was so small he could have put it in a matchbox. But then the rat started to grow."

"Wow," I gasped.

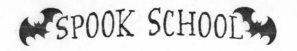
Spookmaster gave a frown. He didn't like to be interrupted. "The rat went on growing until it was much bigger than any normal rat. A terrified Tim ran screaming from the room, but when he returned with his parents the rat had gone. Last night Tim saw this rat-beast again. Once more it started off very small and then began to grow. This time, Tim yelled for his parents to come and see, but even though it was still there when they arrived, they couldn't see it and thought he was imagining it. It seems only children can see this ghostly rat."

"That's unusual, isn't it?" said Lewis.

"Highly unusual," agreed Spookmaster, "and it makes me very

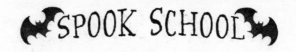

angry, too. Ghosts should never deliberately scare any human, but to pick on a child is very bad indeed. Understandably, Tim is very scared about being on his own, as he thinks this ghostly rat will appear again. And he has no idea why he's being haunted. Tonight, his friend Susie is going to watch for the ghost with him. I want you two to be there as well."

"Excellent," I cried.

"But undercover, of course," said Spookmaster. "We don't want them to know you're there. You only show yourselves to humans in emergencies. To do this, you say, 'See me—'"

"Teachers were always writing that in my exercise books," I quipped, and

then, seeing Spookmaster's stern face,
I whispered, "Sorry."

"You say, 'See me' twice," he went
on, "and then the name of the human
you wish to see you. But on no account
are you to shape-change. You need a lot
more practice to do that properly. And
the moment you shape-change, every
single human can see you."

"We won't," I promised.

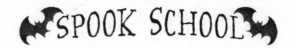

"And one last thing," Spookmaster continued, "we already have a suspect in this case – a ghost who's been known to scare humans in the past. Ghosts such as this are known as creepies."

"Good name for them," I murmured.

"There is a creepy living quite near Tim in Marlow. He's called Oswald and often turns into an ogre. But he's never shape-changed into a rat before. He also claims to have given up haunting people, but he is still our number one suspect. Do not get into a fight with him, though. Is that clear?"

Lewis and I both nodded.

"I just want you to find out which ghost is scaring this boy and politely ask it to stop," said Spookmaster.

"Then come and report to me. Lewis, you are in charge of this mission. And that means you, Charlie, must do as you are told. Do you understand?"

"Absolutely," I said. "And I'd never argue with Lewis about anything."

Lewis gave a laugh, which he quickly turned into a cough.

"You'll be leaving for Earth in a few hours' time when it begins to get dark," said Spookmaster. "Top Ghoul will give you your final instructions. In the meantime, try and get some sleep."

Of course, that was impossible. Lewis and I were far too excited. In the dorm we just couldn't stop talking about the mission, and ended up waking everyone else with our noisy chatter.

But at last it was time for us to leave.
All the other spooks gave us a typical
send-off and let out a huge howl. Then
Top Ghoul told us Tim's address. "Say,
'Spook-travel' and think hard about
where you're going," she said.

Lewis grinned. "Do you know, I've
got a feeling this will be a mission we'll
never forget."

And it certainly was.

Chapter Five

The Rat-beast Returns

We landed outside Tim's house at six o'clock, right in the middle of a huge, great storm. Bolts of lightning shot across the sky. Thunder rolled and rumbled, and the wind howled.

Opposite Tim's house was a large park. I expect normally it would have been full of children playing on the swings and kicking footballs, but this evening it was totally deserted.

Lewis and I talked about the mission while we waited for Susie to arrive. The rain lashed down around us, but being spooks, it just glided through us and we didn't even get a tiny bit wet.

"Hey, look," said Lewis, pointing towards Tim's house. Upstairs we saw an anxious-looking boy peering out of the window.

"That must be Tim," I said.

Then a car pulled up outside his house, and a girl splashed out under a huge umbrella.

"And that must be Susie," said Lewis.

We watched as she sloshed up Tim's drive. She was about to ring the doorbell when someone called out, "Susie! Susie! Please wait."

She whirled round and there was this small boy wearing about four scarves and a funny pointed hat, rushing towards her. "Susie, why won't you at least talk to me?" he cried.

"Because you did a mean and nasty thing. Don't try and deny it. You were caught red-handed."

"But Susie, you've got to listen…"

"No, I'm sorry, Rhys; you're not my friend any more." And she turned her back on him and rang the doorbell. For a moment he looked very hurt. Then he pulled his hat right down over his face and shuffled off to the park.

"I wonder what bad thing he did," I said. "Shall I go and talk to him?"

Lewis stared at me. "Spookmaster said we could only show ourselves to humans in emergencies. And this isn't an emergency. Anyway, that boy is nothing to do with our mission – we're here to sort out the rat-beast. And I'm in charge," he added.

"I know that, but—"

"And I say we go and check on Tim," said Lewis firmly.

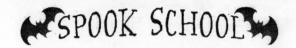

"All right," I said. "I just thought…" But Lewis was already flying towards the window of Tim's room. "Haven't you forgotten something?" I called.

"What?" he said.

"Humans can't see ghosts – unless ghosts want them to, but—"

"They can hear us unless we say 'Spook-silent'," interrupted Lewis. He said it twice and so did I.

We flew into Tim's bedroom. It was a typical boy's bedroom full of books and computer games. The walls bristled with sports certificates and photos of his football team (Chelsea, sadly).

Nothing at all spooky here. And not the kind of place you'd imagine a ghost haunting.

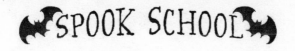

We settled on top of the wardrobe just as Tim and Susie burst through the door. "Guess who's outside your house right now?" said Susie. "Rhys."

"What did he want?" asked Tim crossly. He was quite a tall boy with brown hair and dark eyes.

"I didn't wait to find out," said Susie. "I don't want to be friends with him any more. He stole from me."

"So that's what he did," I hissed.

"If he'd just admitted it we might still be friends," said Susie. "But even when my mobile was found in his locker—"

"Oh, never mind him," interrupted Tim. "I've got more important things to worry about. I'm being haunted by a terrifying ghost."

"I don't believe in ghosts," said Susie.
"In fact, I'm certain they don't exist."

Lewis and I grinned at each other.

"I wonder what Susie would say if
she knew there were two ghosts in this
room right now," I cried. And I flew
down and blew into her ear. She
jumped. Lewis giggled. Then I blew
down her other ear. Her
whole face flinched.

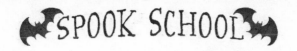

"Are you all right?" asked Tim.

Susie gave a tiny gulp. "I'm fine."

Lewis was really laughing now.
"I'll move some CDs about," I said.

"Go on then," chuckled Lewis. But a second later he cried out, "What are we doing? We're not here to mess about. We're here to solve a mystery."

"Can't we do both?" I asked.

"No," said Lewis firmly. "You're acting like a three-year-old again."

"No I'm not," I said, feeling annoyed. "And you were laughing too."

Lewis ignored this. "I'm the boss of this mission and you've got to do what I say. Now, come back here." I flew back on to the top of the wardrobe. Tim and Susie started playing on the computer.

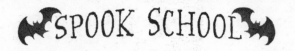

Suddenly Susie said, "It's quite cold in here, isn't it?"

Tim nodded. "The air's gone all chilly. That's a sure sign a ghost is nearby."

"Or that there's a terrible storm outside," said Susie firmly. But her voice rose. "Like I said, ghosts only exist in stories." She returned to the computer, and for a moment the only sound was the wind rattling the windows.

"And that's not a ghost trying to get in," said Susie.

"I know," said Tim. "But don't you think the room feels quiet in a weird way, as if something's about to happen."

"Now you're just being silly."

"Listen," hissed Tim. "Don't you hear something?"

SPOOK SCHOOL

Tim got up. Then he froze in horror. He'd heard something. And then, quite suddenly, Lewis and I did, too. It was a tiny chattering noise, like the sound a baby monkey might make.

"Did you hear that?" said Tim.

"No," said Susie, but she looked anxious.

And then, scampering out from behind the bookshelf came the tiniest rat you've ever seen. It was not much bigger than a spider. "It's here," croaked Tim. "Look."

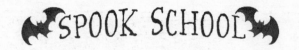

"I can't see anything," cried Susie, but I think she was just pretending.

Then the rat started to grow. Soon it was the size of a large spider. Then it was as big as a mouse.

"You must see it now! You must!" yelled Tim, open-mouthed with horror.

Susie got up and gazed down at the rat as it continued to grow, her expression turning to one of terror.

It was now as big as a terrier, and its eyes had a ferocious gleam.

Meanwhile, that funny, chattering noise grew much louder. In fact, the rat seemed to fill the whole bedroom with its nerve-tingling sounds.

"This is weird," said Lewis.

"Very, very weird," I agreed.

Then Susie let out a piercing scream and fled downstairs. Tim tore after her.

"It's time we did something," said Lewis. "Come on."

I nodded, and let out a little burp. I always do that when I'm nervous.

We flew down towards the rat, which was now the size of a pony. Lewis hovered in front of the beast. "We're the Spook Squad," he said, his voice high and quavery. "And we want you to answer some questions NOW."

Chapter Six

Who Are You?

"First of all," I said, "who are you?"

The giant rat didn't answer.

"Come on, speak," I yelled.

But the rat remained silent. Then, quite suddenly, its paw started to move. Lewis and I both jumped back.

"It's pointing at you," said Lewis.

"I don't care," I said, edging forward again. "And anyway, it's rude to point. Come on, whoever you are, speak to us."

SPOOK SCHOOL

But instead the rat-beast vanished.

"Hey, come back," I shouted. "We haven't finished with you yet."

Just then we heard footsteps rushing up the stairs. Tim and his dad burst into the room, and Mr Webb started opening the drawers and looking under the bed. "If there are any ghosts in here, show yourself now, as I want to finish my tea," he said.

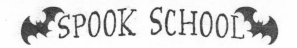

I winked at Lewis. Of course, neither of us moved.

"It's gone now," said Tim.

"I'll just check it's not in here," said Tim's dad, banging open the wardrobe.

"Dad, this isn't funny," said Tim.

Tim's dad put an arm round his shoulder. "Imagination can be a very powerful thing, especially on a night like this. You even scared poor Susie. Come on," he said, "let's go downstairs and I'll make you a nice hot drink."

Lewis and I left, too. We sat outside in the park and waited for midnight so that we could contact Spookmaster (for that's the time when ghosts are at their most powerful). Lewis had to clear his mind and wait for Spookmaster's voice to pop into his head.

Spookmaster listened while Lewis filled him in on our mission so far. He warned us to be very careful, and told us to go to Marlow and interview the number one suspect – Oswald, the ogre.

"Great," I said. "I've always wanted to meet an ogre."

Chapter Seven

Questioning a Creepy

In the end, we didn't fly to Marlow —
we caught the train. It was Lewis's idea.

"It's just I haven't been on a train for
ages," he said. "And I used to love them."

It was after midnight so the train
was pretty empty. Lewis and I stretched
out on the seats while silvery moonlight
lit up the landscape rattling past. "If I
were a ghost on Earth," said Lewis, "I'd
travel on the trains every single night."

"Talk about lazy," I grinned.

We floated off at Marlow station and flew over to Oswald's house. "Now remember," said Lewis, "Oswald is a creepy, and Spookmaster said a creepy needs to be treated with great care. So you'd better let me do all the talking."

"I won't say one single word," I said.

"Perfect," said Lewis.

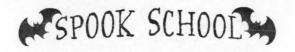

Oswald haunted an old, gloomy-looking house. We flew up the drive and through the door. "Hello, Oswald," called Lewis. "We're the Spook Squad and we've come to interview you."

There was no answer at first and then suddenly we heard a blood-curdling roar that echoed though our ears long after it had finished.

"Now there's a cry to make your hair stand on end," said Lewis. "But it doesn't scare us, does it?"

I pretended not to hear him.

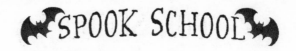

"Oh, come on," said Lewis, "you can speak to me."

"Oh, can I really? Wow, thank you," I said grumpily.

"Stop messing around," said Lewis. "Now, that cry came from the room down there, didn't it?" He pointed down a dark corridor.

"It did."

"Well, off we go," said Lewis. He gave a little gulp. "Come on then."

We floated into a large room which was in total darkness, but of course ghosts can see best in the dark. A fire hissed and crackled, throwing up shadows everywhere. A floorboard creaked all by itself and a huge figure lumbered out of the darkest corner.

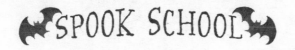

A deep, raspy voice demanded, "Why are you in my house?"

I was looking at the most horrifying, gruesome face I'd ever seen.

He had one eye right in the middle of his face: huge and unblinking. Underneath that was a weird shrunken nose and a massive mouth with disgusting, yellow teeth. There were blotches and pockmarks all over his face, too. But worst of all, was the thing hanging off the end of his nose.

A boil.

A massive grey boil, which looked as if it was about to drop off his face any second. Another boil hung down from his chin. They looked like two decaying apples.

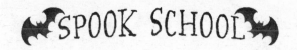

The ogre was so revolting Lewis
and I couldn't stop staring at him.
There was a lot of him to see too, as he
loomed above us.

"What are you two whippersnappers
gawping at? Haven't you ever seen an
ogre before?" His voice rumbled
through the room like thunder.

Lewis and I shook our heads.

"Well, I'm the best ogre you'll ever
clap eyes on. Grisly, ain't I?"

We nodded, lost for words.

"But you can't stay," he said. "I haunt
alone."

"Oh, we haven't come to move in,"
said Lewis quickly. "We're the Spook
Squad and we're here to investigate a
bad thing that's been happening nearby."

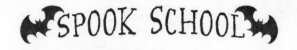

Oswald gave a sharp laugh. "And I suppose you think I've been doing this bad thing?"

"Well, you are a sort of suspect," admitted Lewis. "A ghost has been going to a boy's house and shape-changing into a rat-beast. The boy is called Tim Webb. Do you know him?"

Oswald's eyes bulged at us. Then he let out an ear-splitting cry. "It's not fair, I always get blamed for anything bad that happens."

"The same used to happen to me at school," I said.

"So you know what I mean," said the ogre. "Some people get picked on all the time. And I'm one of them. But I don't know this boy and I've never

been nowhere near him, in fact I've been here every night."

"Can any ghost back up your story?" asked Lewis.

"No, because as I told you, I haunt alone. I've never meant to scare no humans neither. That was all a big misunderstanding. I'm just a ghost who likes being an ogre. It helps keep me cheerful. But I never set out to frighten people. I haunt here very quietly, with just my human, Mrs Pearce."

At that very moment a quivery voice called out, "Oswald, are you there?"

"She calls me most nights," said Oswald. "Gets lonely, you see, and likes me to drop by and say 'Hello'."

"As an ogre?" I asked.

"Oh no," said Oswald, "watch this."
He raised a hand over his face and in
less than a second, he'd changed into a
tall, grey-haired man with a moustache
and a twinkle in his eyes.

"I've never seen anyone shape-change as quickly as that," I said.

"You won't find anyone speedier on Earth," he said proudly. "Now, if you will excuse me for a moment, I must attend to Mrs Pearce."

After he'd gone, Lewis turned to me. "Do you think he's telling the truth?"

"Yeah, I think he is. And I know he's a bit hideous but I sort of like him."

"He can't prove he isn't the rat-beast, though," said Lewis.

"Yeah, but we can't prove he is."

Before Lewis could respond, Oswald returned. "Mrs Pearce is fine now. Unlike most humans, she likes to know there's a ghost about the place. Hang on a moment and I'll change back."

In a flash he was an ogre again. "I've been thinking about your case," he said, as he settled himself on a chair in front of the fire. "I expect you'll be back at this boy's house again tomorrow."

"Yes, we will," said Lewis.

"Well, I've got good news for you; I'm coming along too." Oswald's yellow teeth widened into a smile. Lewis and I gaped at him. "I'm going to help you spooks catch this ghost and prove to you I've got nothing to do with it. So, what's this boy's address?"

Lewis and I looked at each other. Did we really want Oswald to come too?

"Er ... thank you for the offer," said Lewis at last, "but it's best if it's just the Spook Squad there."

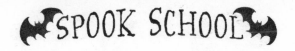

Oswald's voice rose. "But you've got to give me a chance to prove I'm not a creepy. I just get a bit high-spirited sometimes, like you at school, I expect," he said, looking at me. "We don't mean to cause trouble, do we?"

"No, we don't…"

"You and I are very similar, aren't we?" said Oswald to me.

I grinned. "I suppose we are."

"Let me come along." Oswald was just talking to me now. I couldn't help feeling sorry for him, so finally I told him the address. "You'll catch the ghost for certain with an ogre on your side," cried Oswald. "See you tomorrow."

Lewis didn't say a word, but as soon as we got outside he was fuming with rage. "Excuse me, who's in charge of this mission?"

"You are," I said at once.

"So why did you give that ogre the address? I'll tell you why – because you have to show off, don't you?"

"No, it wasn't that," I said. "I suppose I felt a bit sorry for him…"

"You felt sorry for our number one suspect," cried Lewis. "In fact, our only suspect so far. You've done a really stupid thing, Charlie. And that's why I'm taking you off this case."

Chapter Eight

Charlie's Very Last Chance

It was another grey, wet night. All day Lewis had said he was tired and refused to speak to me. Now it was nearly six o'clock and we were outside Tim's house again.

"So you really want me to fly off?" I asked.

"Yes I do," said Lewis.

A few seconds went by. Lewis looked at me. "So why haven't you gone?"

"Well, I just thought that if Oswald really is a creepy, I shouldn't leave you on your own with him, should I?"

Lewis didn't answer; he just floated up into the air away from me.

"Look, Lewis, I'm sorry, all right," I shouted. "And I know you're the boss of this mission. And I won't forget again. But don't make me leave, please."

Lewis swung round. "This is your very last chance, Charlie."

"Thank you," I cried. "And I promise I won't let you down."

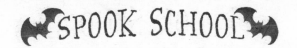

SPOOK SCHOOL

A car drew up, and Susie climbed out. "Honestly, Dad, stop worrying," she said. "Tim and I just scared ourselves last night. We won't see any ghosts tonight. I promise."

She was dashing inside when a voice called out, "Susie."

"It's Rhys," I said, "the boy who was here last night."

"I do know that," said Lewis, who was still in a bit of a mood with me.

"Listen to me, Susie," Rhys cried.

"Just leave me alone," she replied.

"But I'm innocent," he yelled. "It wasn't me. Why won't you believe me?" She didn't answer, and sped into the house.

Rhys sighed heavily. He slowly

73

walked back into the park and sat down
on one of the swings.

"I feel really sorry for him," I said.
"I think he's innocent, too." Then
seeing Lewis's face I added, "But I
know we're on quite a different mission
and I've just got to forget about him."

"Exactly," said Lewis. A nearby
church clock chimed six o'clock.
"Oswald's late."

"No I'm not, you impatient
whippersnappers," boomed a voice.
And there was Oswald.

Lewis and I jumped in surprise. We'd
forgotten what a scary-looking ogre he
was. I couldn't help staring at the boil
hanging off his chin. I was sure it was
even bigger and greyer than before.

"Thanks for coming," said Lewis. "But we don't want humans seeing you."

"Don't worry," said Oswald. "I've already made myself invisible. No human will see or hear me unless I decide to give them a very nasty surprise." He gave a deep laugh. "I wouldn't miss this for the world. I like a good scrap."

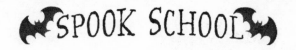

"We're not going to fight the rat-beast," said Lewis, quickly.

"What are we going to do then, shake him by the paw?" asked Oswald raising his hand, which was as big as a spade.

I stifled a giggle.

"No, we're just going to … tell him to stop," said Lewis. "Spookmaster said we mustn't fight him."

"Oh, right you are," said Oswald. "So talking it is then."

Chapter Nine
Ghosts Aren't Real

Lewis and I both said 'Spook-silent'
twice and flew through Tim's window.
A few seconds later Oswald appeared.
He didn't so much fly as waddle. "Not
as swift as you young whippersnappers,"
he grunted.

We settled on top of the wardrobe.
Susie was walking around the room,
saying over and over, "There isn't a
ghost in here."

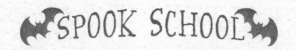

"No, there isn't one ghost, there's three," I grinned. Oswald put back his head and gave a roar of laughter.

"Now you say it," Susie said to Tim.

Tim jumped up and muttered, "There isn't a ghost in here."

"Now believe it," she cried. "Neither of your parents saw it. Why? Because it wasn't really there. We just scared ourselves. Ghosts aren't real, I'm sure."

Oswald gave another loud laugh.

Tim's mum came in with a tray of drinks and chocolate biscuits. "Everything all right?" she asked.

"Oh yes," said Susie firmly.

"Well, don't frighten yourselves again, will you?" she said. "We don't want you having nightmares."

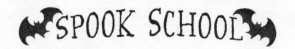

"We won't," said Susie.

"We'll be fine," said Tim. "Bye, Mum." She took the hint and left. We watched as Tim and Susie tucked into the chocolate biscuits.

"I do miss eating food," I said, "especially Easter eggs."

"And ice cream," said Lewis.

"And hot scones bubbling with butter," said Oswald, licking his lips appreciatively. We sat there chatting about our favourite food, while the shadows in the corner of the room grew stronger and deeper.

But there was no sign of the rat-beast.

At last Susie got up. "It looks as if our ghost is having a night off.

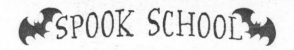
And you know why – because we stopped believing in it. I don't think you'll be seeing the rat-beast again."

Tim grinned with relief. "I know I must have imagined it, but it seemed so real. I really did think I was being haunted." He let out a sigh of relief.

"Oh, I nearly forgot," said Susie. "I saw Rhys again tonight – he's still going on about being innocent."

"Well, maybe…" began Tim. "Maybe…" Then he stopped. He peered outside. "I think it's finally stopped raining," he said quickly. "So why don't we go outside and play football?"

"Good idea," cried Susie.

They tore outside, leaving the three of us still sat on top of the wardrobe.

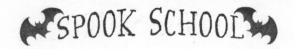

"Well, no rat-beast," said Oswald. "Perhaps I scared it away."

Or perhaps you are the rat-beast. That thought just popped into my head. And I knew Lewis was thinking the same thing. But I really liked Oswald. Surely he couldn't do anything so mean. And why would he keep picking on poor Tim anyway?

"Come on," said Lewis. "Let's go ouside."

The three of us flew out of Tim's window and into the park. The wind was making all the leaves on the trees stir and rustle. They made a strange whooshing sound. No one was about except Tim and Susie, who were having a frantic game of football.

"Hey, you're nearly as good as me," said Tim, smiling.

Susie laughed. "Oh, no one's as good as the great Tim." She gave him a concerned look. "Do you still play football with those older boys…?"

"Not any more," said Tim.

Just then a car pulled up and beeped loudly. "Hey, that's my dad," cried Susie. "I'll see you tomorrow. And remember, there are no ghosts!"

Tim grinned. "I'll remember."

She sped away, leaving Tim to knock the ball about on his own.

"Listen," I whispered suddenly.

All at once the rustling trees seemed to have stopped. Everything was eerily silent except for the sudden cry of a bird as it flew up into the air.

And then we saw something scurry out of the grass. The tiniest rat we'd ever seen.

Tim saw it too. "It's back," he gasped.

Chapter Ten

Oswald's Shocking News

Tim couldn't take his eyes off the rat-beast. It was as if he was hypnotized by it and too terrified to move. Oswald, to my surprise, didn't say anything either. He just let out a shocked grunt.

It was the rat-beast's eyes that were especially scary. They were a deep red and seemed to glitter with hatred.

We watched, horrified, as it grew to the size of a giant dog and raised a huge paw … and this time the paw was pointing right at Tim.

Tim gave a shriek of terror and tore off towards his house. I didn't blame him. It was pretty terrifying. But I felt frightened and angry at the same time. Why was this rat-beast haunting Tim?

"Shall we fight it?" I whispered to Oswald.

He didn't answer. I turned round,
but he'd vanished into thin air.

"Oswald's run away," I said to Lewis.

"Well, we're not going to, are we?"
said Lewis.

"No way," I replied. "It's just a rat
who grows a lot. That's all." I gave
a little burp, then a much louder
one. "So come on."

We flew right up to it.

"Look, this haunting has got to stop," said Lewis, staring right into the fearsome beast's eyes.

"You're really upsetting someone," I added. "A boy who's done you no harm. Come on, speak up, and please stop growing. It's very annoying."

The rat-beast's paw began to move. But instead of anything scary happening, the creature vanished.

"Oh no," cried Lewis, frustrated. "It's gone again."

"We're getting nowhere," I said. "We don't know one thing about this ghost yet."

"Yes you do," said a voice.

It was Oswald, back again.

"Hey, why did you run off like that?"
I demanded.

"I didn't run off," snapped Oswald.
"I had a hunch about something. Now I
know for certain."

"What do you know?" asked Lewis.

"The rat-beast isn't what you think
it is," said Oswald. "In fact, it's not a
ghost at all. It's a trick – a very clever
one done by a magician."

Lewis and I stared at him.

"There are a few magicians on Earth
who have great powers," said Oswald.
"I came across one, once." He shivered.
"Let's say even ghosts shouldn't get
them angry. But I've found the magician
who is doing this. They are never very
far away from their magic. He was

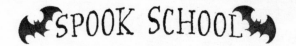

hiding under a tree, while all this was going on. Follow me – but be careful."

We flew deeper into the park.

"Look," shouted Oswald. He was pointing at a figure in the park sitting on a bench under a big oak tree.

I gave a slow whistle.

It was Rhys.

Chapter Eleven

Meeting a Magician

"But he's just a boy," cried Lewis.

"Boy magicians are often the most powerful of all," cut in Oswald.

"I suppose it is a bit of a coincidence, that on both nights we saw the rat-beast, Rhys was lurking about outside," said Lewis. "We must talk to him right away … and this is one time when I believe Spookmaster would say it's OK for us to show ourselves to humans."

"Oh, for certain," I agreed.

"Would you like me to come along with you?" asked Oswald eagerly.

"Well…" began Lewis.

"Don't say another word." His tattered eyebrow drooped over his eye. "I know when I'm not wanted. Best of luck. I'll just wait here for you."

Lewis and I both said, "See me, Rhys" twice, and then flew down to where he was standing. He had his eyes closed and was whispering very faintly, as if chanting a spell.

"Excuse me," said Lewis.

Rhys didn't reply, just went on muttering.

"Excuse me," shouted Lewis. Rhys's eyes shot open.

"Hi there, how are you doing?"
I asked, trying to be friendly.

"I don't know you," he snapped. "Go
away." He turned his back on us and
continued with his chanting.

"We'd like to talk to you about Tim,"
persisted Lewis. "We know you've been
upsetting him with your magic."

A wild look came into Rhys's eyes.
"Yes, I've been upsetting Tim. But he
deserves it. And he's going to get a
return visit later tonight."

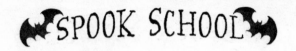

"But you can't just go around scaring people like that," I cried.

"Yes I can," said Rhys, "because I'm a magician. And I can do anything. Poor Tim thinks he's safe from the monster for tonight, but it'll pop up again just when he tries to go to sleep." He started to laugh.

"You're mad," cried Lewis.

"Maybe I am," said Rhys, "in which case you'd better not annoy me or I'll put a spell on you two as well."

"Ah, but we're…" I began. Before I could say another word, a flash of fire suddenly erupted out of the sky and came streaking towards us. I'd never seen such a giant thunderbolt before. It came out of nowhere, taking Lewis and me completely by surprise. And before we knew what we were doing, we were running away as fast as our legs would carry us, with Rhys's mocking laughter echoing in our ears.

We didn't stop until we reached
Oswald, and when we told him what
had happened, we felt really ashamed.
We were angry too – with Rhys, and
ourselves.

"We didn't act like the Spook Squad
at all," said Lewis.

"I know," I said. "Fancy running
away from a thunderbolt…"

I was so mad I couldn't keep still
and neither could my brain. It went on
whirling away, and then I had a brilliant
idea. Oswald liked it right away. "You're
a genius, Charlie," he said.

As for Lewis – well, normally I
don't think he'd have liked my idea at
all, but he was still so furious with
Rhys that he agreed to it, too.

Chapter Twelve

The Ogre Triplets

Lewis and I would fly back to Rhys …
only this time he wouldn't dare ignore
us because we'd have shape-changed into
the scariest creatures he'd ever seen.

Ogres.

Oswald was perfectly happy for us
to copy him. In fact, he took it as a big
compliment. Lewis and I concentrated
really hard and moments later we'd
shape-changed into Oswald-style ogres.

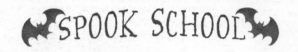

"You'd never think we'd only done one lesson of shape-changing, would you?" I said proudly.

Oswald nodded. "It took me years of practising before I got the hang of it."

Then a horrible thought started to crawl into my mind, as I remembered something Spookmaster had said – on no account were we to shape-change. I really had forgotten that rule until now. And Lewis still hadn't remembered it so I decided not to remind him.

Lewis and I loved being ogres. "Those boils hanging off your face are huge, Charlie, and you look totally revolting."

"So do you," I said.

"Rhys won't laugh at us now." Lewis grinned. "And we'll stop him scaring Tim again … or anyone else."

Oswald gave a husky cough. "Would you boys mind if I ogred along too?"

Lewis hesitated. I knew he'd have preferred it to have been just us two, but it seemed a bit mean not to let Oswald come – especially when we had completely copied the way he looked.

"I do know, Lewis, that you're the one in charge," said Oswald. "And I shall follow your instructions to the letter."

"All right then," agreed Lewis.

Oswald was so pleased he lurched right up into the air and tried to turn a somersault. But halfway he got stuck and had to drop down on to the ground.

The park was empty, except for
Rhys, who was still sitting under the
huge oak tree. As we got nearer we
could hear him chanting a spell.

"Hey, Rat-beast…" I yelled.

And Oswald added, for good
measure, "Hey, Snot-bag."

Rhys whirled round. He opened his
mouth to say something but no sound
came out. We must have really stunned
him. "What … what are you?"

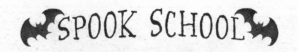

"We're ghosts, who are also known as the ogre triplets," I said. "And we can haunt you for life and turn your limbs to jelly if we want." I was so pleased with my new ogre self. The only slightly disappointing thing was that my voice was the same, and wasn't all deep and raspy like Oswald's.

Then Lewis took over. "We know you've been using your magic to play a cruel trick on someone, haven't you?"

Rhys hung his head, shaking in fear, but he didn't speak.

"Come on, own up, Snot-bag," said Oswald. "I'm just glad you're not a ghost because your behaviour is awful."

"And why did you pick on Tim?" I asked.

"Why?" burst out Rhys so suddenly he made me jump. "Do you know what he did to me?" Before we could answer he rushed on. "Susie had a new mobile phone, the latest model – and Tim stole it. But then he heard there was going to be a search of all our lockers so he panicked and planted the mobile in mine. And when it was found, no one believed me when I said I was innocent. I'd never steal – and certainly not from Susie; she's my friend. Well, she was, but she's not any more, thanks to Tim. No one believes I'm not the thief. I bet even you don't."

There was silence for a moment.

"We might," I said.

"Or we might not," added Oswald.

"You still did a very bad thing to Tim," said Lewis.

"I know," agreed Rhys. "I just didn't know what to do. I've been round to his house and begged him to own up. But he refused."

"So then you put a spell on him," I said.

"For a while I thought I might be a magician. But I only ever did little things before, like conjuring up a bar of chocolate. I've never told anyone either. Not even my mum. But then Tim got me so angry that I decided to frighten him into telling the truth. I remembered him once saying he didn't like rats. So I invented this really terrifying one. I only meant to do it once. But then I watched from outside Tim's house and discovered my spell had worked, and, well, I got a bit carried away…"

"We noticed," I said.

"After that I couldn't stop. It was as if the new power took me over. But I never meant to scare Susie and tonight, I waited until she'd left before I did anything. But Tim deserved it."

"And now you're going to scare Tim again," said Lewis.

Rhys hung his head. "Yeah, my spell was almost ready."

"You have great power," said Lewis, "but you have to be very careful how you use it."

Rhys nodded. "I know." He gave us a puzzled look. "I'm sure I recognize your voices. Aren't you the boys who came to see me before?"

"Yes we are," said Lewis.

"I'm sorry I was so rude," said Rhys, "but by then I was eaten up with anger."

"Well, stop being angry," said Lewis, "because we're going to pay Tim a call now, and persuade him to own up to stealing that mobile."

"Do you think you can?" said Rhys.

"Yes," said Lewis. "But no more scaring people."

After Rhys promised he'd never scare anyone again we left to find Tim.

"We've nearly solved the case," said Lewis. "If Rhys is telling the truth and Tim really did steal that mobile."

"We'll soon find out," I said. "So shall we go as ourselves?"

Lewis nodded. "As much as I like being an ogre, I think we should change back."

Only we couldn't.

"We need to concentrate," said Lewis. But still nothing happened.

"Don't worry," said Oswald, "you'll like being an ogre."

Then Lewis groaned. "I've just remembered something: Spookmaster told us that on no account should we try shape-changing."

"So he did," I said, pretending I'd forgotten until that moment.

"Spookmaster's going to be furious with us," said Lewis.

"Well, with you mainly," I said, "as you're the boss of this mission."

Then Lewis groaned again. "I've just remembered something else. Spookmaster said once we shape-change every single person can see us. So, we'll have to talk to Tim looking like this."

Chapter Thirteen

Three Ogres in a Bedroom

"I really think it's best if Tim doesn't actually see us," said Lewis.

"Yes," I agreed, "it's bad enough seeing ogres outside, but having three of them pop up in your bedroom…"

"…Would really be your worst nightmare," agreed Oswald.

"So we'll just talk to him in the dark," said Lewis.

Lewis and I flew through the

window, followed a few seconds later by
Oswald.

Tim's curtains were drawn and he
was trying to sleep, but he kept sitting
up and thumping his pillow. We
hovered above his bed.

"Hello," whispered Lewis.

Tim sprang up. "Who's there?"

"It's two spooks and a ghost, but
don't worry about that," Lewis said.

Tim seemed very worried indeed
about these new people dropping by.
He sprang up and was about to switch
on the light when Lewis, Oswald and
me all yelled together, "No!"

Lewis added, "Please, whatever you
do, don't switch on the light."

But it was too late. *Click!* The room

was suddenly bathed in light, and Tim got the shock of his life. There in front of him were three ghoulish figures. His mouth dropped open wider and wider.

"Now, don't be alarmed," said Lewis.

"I don't think he can hear you," I cried. "He's in shock."

"Come on, don't be frightened of a few boils," began Oswald. "They're quite good fun. Look, I can make

mine jump." The grey boil on his chin did indeed start springing about.

But Tim remained frozen with terror. And then he began swaying around. "He's going to faint," I cried.

"No, I'm not," said Tim suddenly, "because I know what's happening. This is a dream, isn't it?

I mean, it has to be – three ogres flying about in my bedroom." He laughed loudly. We all laughed loudly, too.

Tim grinned at us. "This is certainly the craziest dream I've ever had."

All three of us laughed again. But then Lewis said, "Actually, Tim, we've come with a very important message. You stole a mobile phone, didn't you?"

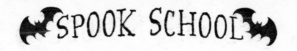

Tim immediately looked away and gazed intently at his carpet. "Don't know what you're talking about."

"Come on, Tim, don't lie in a dream," I said.

"All right, I did take it," he said. "But I didn't want to. There were these three older boys I played football with after school some days. They said I could be in their gang. I thought it'd be cool, but first they wanted me to prove myself by stealing something. They'd seen Susie's new mobile, and told me that's what they wanted. I hated taking it … I knew it was wrong and I knew that those boys were trouble. I don't have anything to do with them any more."

115

"And then there was a big search for the phone," said Lewis, "and you panicked, and planted the mobile in Rhys's locker, didn't you?"

He didn't answer for a few moments but then murmured, "Yes, I did. And I know it was wrong and I'm very sorry. And now I keep seeing this hideous rat-beast – it's like my guilty conscience nagging at me."

"You could well say that," I agreed.

"And now this dream as well," Tim sighed. "I never knew I had such a busy conscience. I'll tell Susie the truth tomorrow. I wanted to tonight, then at the last minute I lost my courage. But first thing tomorrow, I will. You have my promise on that."

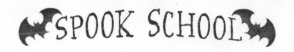

His eyes suddenly closed. "What a mad dream … but I promise, I promise…" Then he fell fast asleep.

We flew out of Tim's room. "We've done it," I cried. "We've solved the mystery and sorted everything out."

"What a relief," agreed Lewis.

Oswald grinned at us. "Why not have another go at shape-changing, because right now I believe you two can do anything."

Lewis and I looked at each other. We concentrated really hard and said,

"Shape-change back", and amazingly we'd shape-changed back to our old selves before we'd even realized it.

"Earlier we couldn't shape-change at all," I said. "But now we did it in about four seconds."

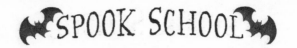

"That's because you believed you could do it this time," said Oswald. "Believe in yourselves and you can do anything."

We were all feeling so pleased with ourselves until I burst out, "But how do we know Tim will keep his promise?"

Lewis thought for a moment. "We'll just have to wait around and see."

So we did. And at eight o'clock the next morning someone going by Tim's house might have spotted three tiny wisps of morning mist drifting past them. They'd never have guessed they were looking at two spooks and a ghost.

Normally Lewis and I would be really sleepy about this time. But not this morning.

120

Around us birds whistled and sung
and squabbled and cars rumbled past.
Then, suddenly, we spotted Susie
striding towards Tim's house.

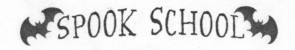

We watched as Tim opened the door and she went inside.

"Shall we slip in there too?" I asked.

"Isn't that a bit nosy?" said Lewis.

"No," I replied.

We were still arguing about this when the door to Tim's house shot open and Susie stormed out.

"He's told her," said Oswald. "Look how mad she is."

She was so angry she didn't see Rhys walking towards her until she nearly bumped right into him. "Rhys, I'm so sorry," we heard her cry. "Tim has just told me that he was the one who stole my mobile…"

At that moment Tim tore out of his house and called over to them.

"Ignore him," said Susie.

"No," said Rhys. "It's time to get this all sorted out."

Susie looked astonished but nodded.

As Tim sped over towards them, Rhys looked away for a moment and murmured, "I wonder if you three ogres are somewhere close by. If you are, thank you. And I promise I'll never use my powers to do bad stuff again."

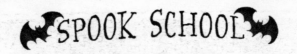

Then we watched Rhys, Tim and Susie all walk off together. "Well, what about that?" said Oswald, happily.

"Oswald, we're going to tell everyone how much you've helped us," said Lewis.

"And how you shouldn't be called a creepy at all," I added.

Oswald couldn't speak for a moment, but both his boils were glowing like lighthouses. "I'm really going to miss you," he said. "In fact, Earth won't seem the same without you. Don't stay away too long, will you?"

"Oh, we'll be back," I cried. "We'll be back before you know it!"

Jokes
(FOR OGRISH FOLK)

> What time is it when an ogre sits on your car? Time to get a new one!

KNOCK KNOCK Who's there?
OGRE! Ogre who?
OGRE THE HILL!

Have you got:

Look out for more Spook School titles coming soon!

And find out more about Pete Johnson at:

www.petejohnsonauthor.com